# WE HAVE OUR FIRST MISSION!

"What's up?" Andrea asked. "You guys look excited."

"Come on," I said as I took off. "We have our first mission!"

We ran around to the front steps so we could talk in private and do our secret handshake without her little brother seeing it.

"We're gonna find out what that little-person homeless-hobo guy is up to," I said. "We need to check out his hiding place for clues."

Andrea and Trish looked at each other.

"His hiding place?" asked Andrea.

"You don't mean the witch's garage, do you?" asked Trish.

"'That's exactly what I mean," I replied. "We're going to do a stake out!"

# UP A CREEK

## A HOLLY HOLLYWOOD FILM ADVENTURE

### BY LINDA ROCKSTROH

**Up A Creek**

**A Holly Hollywood Film Adventure**

by Linda Rockstroh

ISBN: 978-0-692-13059-9

Cover Art by James X. Mackin

Printed by Kindle Direct Publishing

*For my wonderful parents, Ken & Shirley, and for the real Kurt, with love.*

*I am grateful to my mother for teaching me to read and for instilling in me her life-long love of books.*

*Sincere thanks to my editor, Sam Reed, for allowing my book to reach young readers, to my illustrator, James Mackin, for giving Holly physical form, and to my sister Marilyn for her unflagging support and feedback.*

# CONTENTS

# *1*
# ON A BELL

*(On a movie set, a bell rings for quiet. No one should talk or move then, because the filming is starting.)*

"And...ACTION!" I yelled. The film crew standing around behind my Director's chair grew silent.

In the film set in front of me, a door creaked open and a huge hunchbacked figure crept into the darkened living room. A girl lay on the couch, light from the TV flickering across her sleeping face. The hunchback tiptoed up to the couch, an ax blade gleaming in his twisted right hand. He stood over the sleeping girl and slowly raised the ax over her head. Suddenly I heard talking coming from somewhere behind me.

"SHHH!" I said, "We're on a bell!"

If those people didn't stop talking, they would ruin the scene and we'd have to start over. Instead of it getting quiet, there were MORE voices behind me now and they were getting even louder! The actor who played the hunchback looked over at me and the scene was ruined. I had to stop the camera.

"Cut, cut, CUT!" I yelled.

My eyes shot open and I found myself lying in my bed, sunlight streaming through my bedroom window. It was just another Movie Director dream - I had them all the time - but I could still hear the loud voices. I realized it was just my mom and dad, banging around in the kitchen.

I'm Holly Stone, by the way. I just turned ten and I'm headed for the fifth grade. Mom and Dad and I moved this week from the  city of Los Angeles, which we call L.A., to this little town of Lebanon in Indiana. We moved here to Lebanon because the place where Dad worked in L.A., a sporting goods and camping store called "Out and About", decided to open another store in Indianapolis. That's a big city only about a half-hour from here, and it also happens to be the capitol of Indiana. Dad's the General Manager of the new store, which is kind of like being the Director of a movie, since he's in charge.

I was kind of afraid Lebanon would be dull after a big city like L.A., but it turns out I can get in as much trouble in a small town as I can in a big city.

I yawned and stretched and looked around the room. Packing boxes were still stacked along the wall.

I'm not used to my new room yet, since I've only been here three days. It's a cool room, though, with a blue ceiling that looks like the sky. Dad got me some of those glow-in-the-dark stars to put on the ceiling, but I hadn't had time to do it yet.

There's a big closet that connects my room to the room next door. You just walk right through the closet and there you are! I'd like to make the next room into a movie studio, but Mom says it's gonna be the guest room.

My bedroom's upstairs and it faces the front of the house. The front porch roof is right out my window and I'm thinking I might be able to crawl out the window and sit out there, like on a balcony. That'd be great, but I may not mention it to my parents because they'd probably say it was too dangerous. In fact, I'm sure they would, so why worry them?

I decided to unpack and start to get my new room set up, so I opened the first box and found the pack of glow-in-the-dark stars right on top of my stuffed animals. I climbed up on the desk and stood there on my tip-toes, trying to reach the ceiling so I could put the stars up there. I was still too short, so I stuck them on the wall instead, as high up as I could reach. They looked just fine when I finished.

The next box I opened was full of my books, so I started putting them on my bookshelf. After that I didn't get much else done, because I found a really good book I'd started to read back in L.A. and sat down to finish it. Reading is my favorite hobby, next to movie making, and I can read for hours.

The next thing I knew, there was a knock on my bedroom door.

"Holly!" called my mom.

My parents are getting pretty good about knocking before they come in. I mean, now that I'm ten I think I should get SOME respect!

"Here's some sunscreen for you to put on before we go out," Mom said. She was already dressed in shorts and a tank top for the pitch-in.

If you don't know what a pitch-in is, don't feel bad. I didn't know, either, until yesterday. A young couple named Marge and John Smith from down the block had invited us over to meet the neighbors. They said it would be a "pitch-in". We were confused until they explained that a pitch-in was a picnic where each family brings its favorite dish of food for everyone to share. We called that a pot-luck back in L.A.

I put on cut-off shorts with my favorite T-shirt and I slapped on some sunscreen. I took a quick peek in the mirror and smiled. A kind-of-skinny girl with straight kind-of-blonde hair smiled back. I stuck my tongue out. I wiggled my ears. I pushed my nose up so it looked like a pig snout. I got bored, so I made my bed and ran downstairs. Dad was just coming in the backdoor to the kitchen.

"How are my girls doing?" Dad asked.

My mom was taking a dish out of the oven. Dad dropped his keys on the counter and went over to grab her in a big hug.

"Careful! This dish is hot!" she said in a stern voice, but she was smiling like she liked it.

"What did you make?" I asked.

"My spicy tofu casserole," said mom with a smile.

I tried not to make a face. It's not my favorite food, by a long shot!

Mom gets carried away with this health food stuff. Come to think of it, pretty much every body we know back in L.A. is a food nut in one way or another. If they aren't going on about carbs and fat grams, then it's organic foods and gluten-free foods or soy this and tofu that. I don't get it. To me it's just food and it isn't worth hours of conversation! Mom says I just like to be contrary and go against whatever everyone else is saying or doing. She's not all wrong, but I really DO think, "Enough already with the food obsession!"

That's my favorite new word, "obsession". It means something you're hung up on and can't get out of your head. My obsession is making movies. Not all obsessions are bad. I mean, I'm pretty sure Beethoven was obsessed with music and Tiger Woods is obsessed with golf, and see where that got them! I'm gonna be like the first girl Spielberg. He's the most famous movie director in the world, I bet, and that's what I want to be when I grow up.

Dad took the big plaid stadium blanket out of the closet, Mom picked up the casserole, and I ran off to grab the digital camera from the family room. I pretty much don't go anywhere without it. You never know when you'll see something interesting that you could make into a movie.

It turns out it was a good thing I had my camera later that day.  If I hadn't, I might not have seen the weird thing that started this whole adventure.

# *2*
# ROLL IT!

*(The order given to the cameraman
to start filming a scene.)*

The Smiths, that's Marge and John, lived on the corner of our block and had a big backyard with a patio and a jungle gym and a playhouse.

The yard was full of neighbors, grown-ups and kids, and everybody was having a good time. I started to do what I love best. I turned on my camera to get a shot of all the people.

"Roll it!" I said. I liked to say it, even though I didn't need to since I was the one actually turning on the camera this time. With the camera held up to my eye, I started panning the crowd. "Panning" is film talk for moving the camera from side to side so you get a shot of everybody. As I panned the crowd in the yard, I recognized a brown-haired girl, named Trish, who lived two doors down. When her family brought us homemade cookies on moving day, three days ago, I found out Trish was gonna be in my class when we started school in the fall.

"Hey, Holly!" she yelled, waving like mad. "Come on down here a minute!"

Trish yells a lot. She's very enthusiastic.

"Hey, Trish!" I called back.

I turned off the camera and jumped down the patio steps. I always take them two at a time – it's faster that way. I went on over to where Trish had set up camp with her mother, her sister Melanie who was in high school, and a gray-haired woman who sat under a big flowered umbrella.

"This is my Grandma Kurtz," Trish said. "Grandma, meet Holly, the new girl. She just moved here from Hollywood! THE Hollywood, in California!" She poked me in the arm. "Say something in film-talk, Holly!"

I was a little embarrassed. When her family brought cookies over that first day I got a little carried away filming our moving day. When they came to the door I started filming them with the camera and I was saying stuff for the sound track like, "And here are our first new neighbors, arriving to welcome us to town." Then I pointed at them and yelled, "Action!" That meant they were supposed to start talking so I could get it all on camera, but they just stood there with their mouths open 'til my mom came up behind me and snatched the camera out of my hands.

"Oh, Holly, leave them alone a minute," my mom had said. "Let these nice people get in the door and say hello before you start putting them in your movies!"

I was pretty humiliated, which was my new word for the day that day. It meant I was really, really embarrassed in front of other people.

Trish poked me again. I had spaced out for a minute and her whole family was looking at me.

"Come on, talk film for us!"

"Uh, not now, Trish."

I smiled at her grandmother and stuck out my hand to shake.

"Nice to meet you Mrs. Kurtz," I said.

"It's very nice to meet you, too, Holly," said her grandma. "It'll be fun for Trish to have a friend on the block."

She opened up a Tupperware container and held it out it to me.

"Would you like a lemon bar? They're Trish's favorites, so I made them this morning. Have two, if you want!"

"Thank you. They look delicious," I said as I picked one out.

I took a bite. Yum!

"What have you got there?" asked my mom as she and Dad came over to us.

"Trish's grandma made it. It's a lemon bar. Try a bite," I said and held it out for her to taste.

She took a bite and then let out a little "Mmmm!" before she caught herself and said, "Do you know how bad this is for you? It tastes like pure butter and sugar!"

"Yeah," I replied. "It's great, isn't it?"

Of course, then my dad wanted to taste it. After he took a bite he gave me a big grin and a secret wink.

The people at the pitch-in all seemed to know each other. I felt a little left out since we didn't know anybody yet, and it made me miss L.A. My mom told me that I'd have no trouble making new friends here since I was a nice outgoing girl, but I still felt sad about leaving all of my old friends behind.

I decided right then and there that my next movie would be called "My New Hometown". When it was done, I'd send it to the friends back in L.A. so they could see where I live now.

"Let's get out of here," Trish said. "I want to show you a really rad secret place I know."

She grabbed my hand and we ran over to my parents so I could get permission to leave the pitch-in.

"Hey," I said as I skidded up to her and Dad. "We're gonna go exploring for a while, okay?"

"All right," said my dad, "but be back in half an hour. We'll be eating then."

"All right," said my mom, "But be careful and stay out of trouble."

I swear my mom can tell the future. How did she know I was going to get into trouble?

# *3*
# THE ANTAGONIST

*(The bad guy in a movie.)*

I grabbed my camera by the carrying strap, and Trish and I were off down the sidewalk at a run. I don't know why we were running except that it was a beautiful day and running just felt good.

"Do you take that camera everywhere?" asked Trish as she ran.

"Yep," I said. "I might want to shoot some stuff for the movie I'm making. Making movies is what I do."

"Then I'm gonna call you Holly Hollywood," said Trish. "That'll be your nickname."

I thought that was pretty cool. Holly Hollywood was a good name for a movie director.

"Follow me!" yelled Trish, as she skidded around a corner and into an alley.

Trish's brown ponytail bobbed as she ran, and I was so close behind her that when she stopped suddenly I smacked right into her and we both fell down. When Trish landed she let out a fart that sounded like a cross between a "honk" and a "tweet". I was gonna be polite and ignore it, but Trish just sang out "Beans, beans, the musical fruit. The more you eat the more you toot!" We started laughing our heads off and rolling around on the ground making tooting sounds.

When we got a grip on ourselves and stood up again, I saw we were right next to a little river or stream or something.

"This is the creek," said Trish. It runs all through town. I play down here all the time."

"Cool!" I said.

I slid behind her down the little bank right to the edge of the water. The water wasn't very deep – maybe knee deep in the middle – but it was moving along pretty well, over the rocks and sticks and clumps of grass that were sticking out here and there.

She led me along beside the water until we got to a very shallow kind of cove with a miniature beach.

"Look here," said Trish. She pointed to five big stones in the water.

"Here's how I get across to the other side," she said.

I noticed that the rocks made a kind of zig-zag path across the creek, but they looked pretty far apart.

"Watch me," said Trish. "I'll show you how you have to do it so you don't fall in. You have to step on each rock just a certain way so they don't tip."

She jumped onto the first rock and waved her arms to keep her balance.

"Let me get a shot of it for my movie," I said.

I squatted down and started filming. When I was looking through the camera to get a shot of the water rushing past the stepping-stones, I saw a flash of something moving on the far creek bank. I looked again.

"Shhh!" I said. "See over there across the creek? I think there's somebody spying on us!"

Trish stared open-mouthed at the spot where I pointed. There was movement in the bushes and we saw a really short guy scramble away along the bank toward a bridge that crossed the creek. He had on a black stocking cap and layers of old clothes – it looked like a wrinkled sport coat over a dirty sweatshirt and baggy brown pants rolled up a bunch at the ankles. We didn't get a really good look at him because of all the bushes on that side.

23

"It looks like a homeless midget or a midget hobo or something!" Trish said in a loud whisper.

"They're called "little people", not "midgets", I replied. "My mom says "midget" isn't a nice word."

"Well, what do you think that little-person homeless hobo guy was doing down here?" asked Trish.

"I don't know," I said. "He was acting awful sneaky. Maybe we should just go back to the pitch-in."

To tell you the truth, I was a little spooked.

We walked back along the creek to where it went under a bridge with a low cement wall to keep people from falling into the creek from the sidewalk up above. We were getting ready to climb up the bank to the sidewalk when Trish let out a squeal that about broke my eardrums. A girl our age skipped onto the bridge above us. She had really short hair and wore glasses, which had slipped down to the end of her nose. She pushed them back up with her middle finger.

"Hey, Trish," said the girl. She went around the side of the bridge and started down the bank of the hill towards us. She slipped and ended up sliding down on her butt. We got a good laugh out of that. Her glasses were down on the end of her nose again so she poked them back up with her middle finger.

"This is my best friend Andrea," said Trish. "She lives over by the cemetery on the way to school."

"Holly just moved here from L.A.," she said to Andrea. "Her nickname's "Holly Hollywood" because she makes movies."

"Cool!" said Andrea around the big wad of gum she was chewing. She blew a huge bubble and popped it with a big bang.

That made us all grin. She had a nice smile, although it was covered in sticky pink now.

"Darn!" she said, as she tried to peel the gum off of her face. "I guess three pieces at once is too many!"

We all laughed, and she gave us some gum, too.

"What are you guys doing?" she asked.

"I'm gonna show Hollywood the secret hiding place," said Trish.

"You can't tell anyone about it," warned Andrea.

Then we were under the bridge which formed a kind of tunnel over the creek, in our own little world, and the people up top couldn't see us.

"This is really cool!" I said.

I started filming while Trish and Andrea went over to a stump by the bridge wall and reached in behind it.

"This is our instant hut," said Trish.

She and Andrea pulled out what looked like a huge piece of cardboard and laid it on the ground by the water.

When they unfolded it and stood it up, I saw that it was a giant box that looked like a house with double doors. From the big printing on the side of the box, I could tell that it had once had a refrigerator in it.

"I just LOVE this!" I said. "It's a perfect hideaway!"

We all crawled in and pulled the two door-flaps closed behind us. It was kind of dark that way, so we opened them back up.

"I think we should form a secret club," I said, "and this will be our secret clubhouse!"

"Yeah, and we can have a secret password and everything!" said Trish.

We started trying to come up with a name for the club. We tried names with "three" in them, like "Secret Three" or "Three for All." We talked about using our initials to make the name, which would be "HAT", for Holly, Andrea, Trish. We decided that if we used those names, though, we couldn't ever let someone new into the club – if anybody who was secret-club-member material ever came along.

Then I remembered about how you can make a new word from the first initials of other words that go together, like the group called MADD, which is "Mothers Against Drunk Driving", so we tried that.

It was hard, and we came up with mostly dumb names like "FUB", for "Friends Under Bridge". Finally, I remembered one of my dad's favorite sayings – "A friend in need is a friend indeed." So we came up with "FINS", for "Friends in Need Society", and our secret club was born.

We invented a secret handshake that goes like this: you stick your hands out like you're going to just shake hands, but you grab each other's wrists instead. You give three shakes like that (since there are three of us) and then slide your hands down 'til you just hook pointer fingers, and you give three shakes that way. Finally, you waggle your leftover fingers like fins – or, I guess I should say, like FINS.

"Now it's time to fix up our official club house," I said. "Let's make a front yard with some grass and plants and rocks."

I crawled out first, and that's why I was the one to spot him. It was the little-person homeless hobo, and he was down the creek by our miniature beach, looking right our way.

"It's HIM!" I squealed. Trish and Andrea pushed their way out behind me.

We all grabbed each other's hands and squealed some more, and he crouched down and started to run away.

"Let's follow him!" I said. "He's up to something, and it can't be good! Hurry up!"

I tucked my camera under my arm and we scrambled along the bank, following his trail. He was pretty far ahead of us, but we were fast. We crawled up the bank right where we saw him go, and spied him running down the street and into an alley. When we got to the end of the alley we saw him duck into a rickety little old garage.

It was really more of a shack than a garage, and it was leaning to one side. It was tacked together from weathered old wood, and all the paint had worn off. The windows were broken and the doors were all crooked.

Trish grabbed my arm. "Stop right here!" she said in a loud whisper. "That's the witch's yard!"

Andrea nodded her head and looked really spooked.

"A witch lives there?" I asked, my eyes wide.

"She lives in that house," said Andrea, pointing across the weed-infested yard. "And that's her garage. We never go near it!"

It was hard to believe that a witch lived on our block, but Trish and Andrea had lived here a long time, so I figured they must know.

"Uh-oh!" I said, looking at my watch. "We've been gone a half hour already, and we're gonna get in trouble if we don't get back to the pitch-in! My dad's real big on punctuality."

Punctuality means being on time, and it's one of my dad's favorite words.

"We've got to put away the clubhouse first," said Trish, turning to go. "If we leave it out, someone might steal it!"

We ran back and folded up the big box, hiding it behind the stump again. We dashed back to the pitch-in as fast as we could, but we were 5 minutes late, anyway.

"Don't tell anybody about our mystery man," I said as we skidded into the back yard. "We're gonna figure this out on our own, or we're not FINS!"

# *4*
# CRAFT SERVICE

*(A big table full of snacks and food for the
film crew to eat all day while they work.)*

We split up to join our families. My parents were
just dishing out some food for themselves, so I slid in
beside them and grabbed a plate. I don't think they
even noticed I was late.

We filled our plates with the different kinds of
food everybody had made, and found a place at a
picnic table with another family. The little boy in that
family was picking all the peas out of his seven-layer
salad. He was making a little pile of them by his plate.

Everybody ate a bunch of food and went back
for seconds. I was glad to see that they finished off my
mom's tofu casserole.

When it started to get dark, I noticed little tiny
blinking lights over by the bushes at the side of the
yard. They were floating in the air.

"What are those floating lights?" I asked

A lady at our table looked over her shoulder to where I was pointing.

"Oh, those are just lightning bugs. Don't you have those in California?"

We sure didn't. She explained that they were flying bugs with a chemical or something that made them glow in the dark. There were more of them now, blinking on and off.

Andrea and Trish rushed over to me. Andrea had a big spot on her shirt where she'd spilled something on herself.

"Let's catch some lightening bugs and put them in a jar!" yelled Trish. "I can put it by my bed, like a nightlight!"

She grabbed an empty mustard jar that was sitting on the picnic table, and we ran over to rinse it out with the garden hose.

"We need holes in the lid, so they can breathe," said Andrea.

I knew my dad carried a pocketknife so we had him poke some holes for us.

"Let me carry the jar," said Andrea. She added some grass in the bottom of it.

"Let's go!" yelled Trish. She was hopping up and down.

She caught the first lightning bug and ran over to Andrea.

"Take the lid off," said Trish.

Andrea unscrewed the lid and Trish popped the lightening bug into the jar. As soon as she did, though, Andrea dropped the lid and the jar and the bug got away. I was beginning to see that Andrea was kind of accident-prone. I took over the jar-holding job.

"I got one!" called Andrea.

She ran over and put it in our jar.

"All RIGHT!" yelled Trish, and she high-fived Andrea. Trish's excitement was contagious, which means you can catch it from her, like a cold. It was one of the things I really liked about her.

After that we caught a bunch more of the blinking bugs. They were pretty amazing, with their bodies glowing on and off. I'd never seen anything like them! I tried to film some of them for my movie, but I wasn't sure if it would turn out since it was so dark outside.

The mosquitoes came out, too, so everybody started packing up to leave.

Mom and Dad held hands all the way home, so I walked behind them, being careful not to step on the cracks in the sidewalk. You know, because of the old saying, "Step on a crack you'll break your mother's back." I don't really believe that, but why take a chance?

# *5*
# CLIFFHANGER

*(When you leave a mystery at the end of*
*a scene, so people want to know more.)*

The next day, after breakfast, I asked Mom if I could go play with Trish and Andrea.

"I'm glad you already have two new friends," said Mom. "Go on and have fun, but let me know where you'll be if you decide to leave the block."

I grabbed my camera and ran down to Trish's house. When I knocked on the back door, she was just finishing her Froot Loops so I got a shot of her on tape for the "My New Hometown" movie. Then I sat down with her and ate a few handfuls out of the box.

"Do a commercial," I said. "Say what you like about the cereal." I turned on my camera and said "Action!"

"Froot Loops are the best!" she said. "I eat them every day and they make me see colors better!"

Trish has one wacky imagination!

When she was finished eating, she rinsed out her cereal bowl and left it in the sink.

"Let's head on over to Andrea's. It's on the next block," Trish said.

"Mom!" she yelled before I could say anything. "We're going down to Andrea's house!"

She ran out the back door, and I was right behind her.

What the heck, I thought, it would only be for a minute and Mom would never know.

When we knocked on Andrea's front door her mom said she was out in the back yard, so we went on around. She was eating gummy worms and watching her little brother Todd dig a hole. I got a little of the digging on camera for my movie, just in case. Maybe he'd find treasure or something.

"What's up?" Andrea asked, pushing her glasses up on her nose.

She kind of mumbled, since her mouth was full.

"Come on," I said as I took off. "We have our first mission!"

"Is it a dangerous mission?" asked Andrea.

"Nah," I said. "It's an exciting mission, like in an action movie!"

We ran around to the front steps so we could talk in private and do our secret handshake without her little brother seeing it.

"We're gonna find out what that little-person homeless-hobo guy is up to," I said. "We need to check out his hiding place for clues."

Andrea and Trish looked at each other.

"His hiding place?" asked Trish.

"You don't mean the witch's garage, do you?" asked Andrea.

"That's exactly what I mean," I replied. "We're going to do a stake out!"

I told them that a stake out is when the cops hide outside a bad guy's house and watch to see what he does.

"My Uncle Kurt explained it to me. He's a cop back in L.A.," I said, hoping that I didn't sound like a know-it-all.

"You're crazy!" said Andrea. "We told you a WITCH lives in that house! We don't know what she would do to us if she caught us hiding in her yard."

"Yeah!" added Trish. "She might turn us into frogs or something! Or maybe she'll give us warts or make our teeth all fall out!"

"Come on, you guys," I said. "It'll be okay. We'll check out her house first, to make sure she's not outside where she could see us."

We started off down the street to the witch's house. I felt better once we got back on my own block, where I was supposed to be.

When we got to the sidewalk in front of the witch's house we all stopped and kind of huddled up together. I admit I was a little scared.

"How do you even know she's a witch?" I asked in a whisper.

"Just look at her house!" said Trish.

The front yard was so covered with weeds and vines that you could hardly see the house. It made the porch look kinda dark and spooky. The house itself wasn't even really painted, but was an old grayish-brown. Some of the railings on the front porch were broken off like rotten teeth, and the windows were covered with old newspaper on the inside. I have to admit, it DID look like a witch's house.

I started to film it for my movie. My friends back in L.A. would be so envious that I had a witch living on my block!

I was just zooming in on the house when a huge scruffy old black cat came slinking up onto the porch from around the side. Half its tail was missing, and when it turned our way I saw that it only had one eye! There was just a big scar where the other eye had been. I freaked out and took off running. The other girls were right behind me.

We stopped down the block and I bent over to catch my breath.

"That's a witch's house, if I ever saw one!" I panted. "There's even a black cat!"

"I heard that her cat killed a neighbor dog," said Andrea. "You don't want to get near it!"

"Okay," I panted. "Okay, we'll have to watch out for the cat AND the witch. We'll do our stake out from the back alley."

They both looked at me like I was crazy, but they followed me back to the alley. We were the FINS, after all, and we had to stick together.

We sneaked down the alley behind the witch's house, going from one hiding place to another and trying to be quiet.

Andrea kicked an old can that was on the ground and that made a pretty big sound. Then she said "Oh, fudge!" pretty loud, but other than that we did okay.

When we got to a place where we could see the old garage, we looked for a hiding spot for our stake out.

"Behind here!" Trish whispered loudly. "I think we'll all fit."

She wiggled her way behind a fence covered with vines. We squeezed in beside her and all ducked down. It was a pretty good spot, once we made holes through the vines so we could see out.

Stakeouts are really pretty boring. You just sit there and wait for something to happen and you have to stay quiet the whole time, so you can't really play games or talk to make the time go faster. We were all getting pretty sick of it, and hungry, too, when Andrea grabbed my arm.

"Look! Here he comes," she whispered.

She pointed down the alley and sure enough, here he came.

I tried to get a shot of him with my camera, but a vine got in my way at the last minute and Andrea still had a hold of my arm, so the camera kept jiggling.

The little-person homeless hobo was sneaking along, kind of crouched over. He gave a quick look around, and then slipped into the witch's garage.

"Now what?" asked Trish. This was her first stake out.

"Well," I said. "Well, now we, um… now we, uh…"

I slapped my ankle, like a mosquito had just bitten me, in order to have a minute to think. This was my first stake out, too.

"Now we just watch, and when he comes out we follow him!"

"I sure hope he comes out soon," whined Andrea. "This is getting boring."

Right then the guy poked his head out the door and looked all around. We ducked way down so he wouldn't see us. When he slipped out the garage door we saw that he had a cigar box tucked under his arm.

Was it stolen money? Was it the witch's spells? Was it a bomb? My imagination was going wild and I just had to know!

# *6*
# COMIC RELIEF

*(When something funny happens to give
a break from the tension in a scene.)*

"Let's go!" I said. "We have to keep him in
sight!"

"And don't kick the can this time, Andrea," said
Trish as we sneaked after him. Andrea stuck out her
tongue at Trish.

We followed him up one alley and down
another, hiding behind whatever we could find along
the way. We hid behind a garbage can, a big lilac bush,
and a rusty old car.

He crossed the street to the next block. He was
running and I didn't want to lose him, so I just dashed
across the street with my friends.

He took a shortcut through a yard by going
behind their bushes along the fence, and we did the
same thing. That was where Andrea stepped in a pile of
dog doo.

"Oh, Yuk!" she said. "Look what I stepped in!"

Trish held her nose and backed into me, almost knocking me over.

"Watch it, you guys!" I said, as I bent over to find a stick so that Andrea could clean the mess off of her shoe.

I wasn't hiding in any more small spaces with her 'til she got that doo doo all cleaned off!

"Here," I said, giving her a good cleaning stick. "I'm gonna try to catch up with him before he gets away. You guys get cleaned up and then follow."

I ran on out of there, keeping an eye out for more dog doo, and got a glimpse of our mystery guy cutting through some bushes into another yard. I stopped behind the bushes and turned on the camera to get a shot of him. That's when I got hung up in the branches and almost dropped the camera.

When I finally looked through the bushes, I saw a door in the side of the house swing shut. It looked like the door to a basement to me. We had a door just like that at my house.

I was standing there with my mouth open when Andrea and Trish came up behind me and grabbed my arms.

"What happened?" asked Andrea.

"Where is he?" asked Trish. "Did you lose him?"

"I don't know," I said slowly. "I THINK he might have just sneaked inside that house!"

"Oh, my gosh!" they both said.

We stared at each other in amazement. This was serious.

"Wow!" said Trish. "Do you really think he went inside?"

"I'm not sure," I said, "but I saw the door swing shut, and I didn't see him anywhere after that."

"Maybe we'd better tell the police or our parents or somebody," said Andrea.

I thought about that for a minute. A guy hiding in somebody's run-down old shack of a garage wasn't too bad, I figured, but sneaking into someone's home was different. I mean, what if he were a robber or a bad guy of some kind? I really didn't want to tell my parents, though, since I hadn't told my mom I was gonna be on that block!

"Okay, let's think about this a minute," I said. "I'm not even SURE he went into that house. Why don't I just talk to my Uncle Kurt in L.A. and tell him about it? He'll know what to do, since he's an actual policeman."

"That's a good idea," said Trish. "You're just guessing where he went, anyway, since you didn't really SEE him. No need to upset our parents 'til we're sure. Let's see what your Uncle Kurt has to say about it first."

We agreed that I'd go home and call my uncle. I'd have to do it in secret somehow, or my parents would want to get on the phone with him, too. Then he'd tell them why I called, and I'd probably get grounded for a month!

We were a serious bunch of FINS when we did our secret handshake and split up for home.

We had my favorite foods that night - macaroni and cheese  and fresh broccoli. I couldn't totally enjoy my dinner, though, since I felt bad about keeping a secret from my mom and dad.

After we ate I went straight up to my room and closed the door. I didn't think I could get away with making a secret phone call to my Uncle Kurt since our only phones were in the kitchen and in my parents' room, so I came up with Plan B. Plan B was to E-mail him from my computer. I liked this plan, because then

Uncle Kurt couldn't get into a big lecture like he might over the phone.

I turned on the computer and started typing. I'm not very good at it. I think I use about four fingers in all when I type, which I know isn't what you're supposed to do, but what the heck. It just takes a little longer that way. Here's what I ended up sending:

*Hi, Uncle Kurt.*

*How R you? How's L.A. doing without me? I have a question for you, since you're a cop. What if a person thinks he or she might have seen someone sneak into someone else's house? The person's not sure, but he or she thinks that a little-person homeless hobo sneaked into a stranger's house. What should the person who might have seen this do???*

When I read it over I thought it was a little confusing, and that it sounded pretty much like I was the person I kept talking about, even though I used "he or she" to try and hide it. I probably wasn't fooling him. He IS a cop, after all, and they're not that easy to fool! I sent it anyway, since I couldn't think of a way to fix it.

I wrote some E-mails to my friends back in L.A., too, and told them I'd be sending them the "My New Hometown" movie pretty soon. Writing to them made me miss them, but I told them I was making new friends. By the time I was finished, I had an E-mail back from my uncle. This is what it said:

*Hey, Holly!*

*It was good to hear from you, but the question you asked has me a little worried. If a person really saw someone sneaking into someone else's house, then what she saw is called "breaking and entering". That's an actual crime, Holly, and the police should be involved. The person, especially if it happens to be a young girl, should NOT be involved. I KNOW you're talking about yourself, Holly. I AM a cop, after all, and not that easy to fool You say you're not sure this really even happened, though, and I know you have an active imagination, so maybe you should just drop it and stay away from strangers or I'll have to call your parents.*

*Love U and miss U, Uncle Kurt*

Well, it was a long E-mail. I guess Plan B didn't save me from a lecture after all, but I kind of asked for it. I printed it out to share with the FINS tomorrow, and shut down my computer.

It was past my bedtime.

# *7*
# SUBPLOT

*(Something that happens outside the main story,*
*that tells you more about the main character.)*

A turtledove woke me with its "coo, coo, coo" sound. The sun was pouring in the window. I looked around my nice new room and felt pretty good. I had decided in my sleep, somehow, to take my Uncle Kurt's advice. After I told the FINS what my uncle said, we'd just drop the whole thing. It was a load off my mind. After breakfast I was eager to get together with the club, but my mom reminded me that I still hadn't finished unpacking the boxes in my room.

"I need to get all the moving boxes out to the curb for trash pick-up," she said.

"Well, could Trish and Andrea come over to help me?" I asked. "It'll be faster that way."

"Sure," she said. "But you're not leaving the house until I get those boxes!"

When Trish and Andrea arrived we ran upstairs to get the job done. I had Trish unpack the box with my plastic monster models in it, since I was afraid Andrea might break them. I hate to say it, but sometimes she's kind of clumsy.

"Did you put all these models together yourself?" asked Trish as the put them on the shelf.

"Yeah," I said. "They're monsters from my favorite horror movies."

We messed around with the models for a while, setting them up in scenes that I filmed with my camera.

"Let's finish this and go outside," said Andrea. "All these monsters kind of give me the creeps."

"Hey!" I said. "Let's go outside right here!"

I opened the window, the one that opens onto the front porch roof. Then I took out the screen window.

"What are you doing?" asked Trish. She and Andrea came over to look out.

"We can climb out here and see the world!" I said. I put one leg over the windowsill and started to climb out on the roof. Andrea grabbed my other leg to stop me.

"We better not," she said. "It looks dangerous!"

"No, it'll be great!" yelled Trish.

I shook my leg loose from Andrea and climbed out. Trish was right behind me. We view was fantabulous! That's a word I made up for really good stuff. It means fantastic and fabulous all rolled into one.

"Hey!" yelled Trish. "It's like we're princesses looking down on our kingdom from up on the castle tower!"

"Not so loud, Trish," I said. "Mom will hear us."

Andrea poked her head out the window.

"You guys better get back in here," she said. "I think I maybe hear her coming upstairs right now."

Trish and I scrambled back into my room and I put the screen back in the window.

"Grab a box!" I hissed. "Try to look busy!"

It turns out my mom wasn't coming up the stairs, after all. I'm pretty sure Andrea just said that to get us to come in off the roof. We were making her nervous, being out there. I think she was afraid we'd fall off or something.

We finished unpacking in a hurry. When we were done, we slid the empty boxes down the stairs to my mom and we were free at last!

I grabbed my camera and we ran outside.

"We need to go to the clubhouse and have a FINS meeting," I said. "It's important business."

We headed down to the creek together. We got the clubhouse out of its hiding place, put it together, and climbed in. I showed them my Uncle Kurt's E-mail.

"You don't think he'll tell your parents, do you?" asked Andrea

"Nah," I said. "He won't, if we just drop it right now."

"Good," said Trish. "Then that's what we'll do.

We shook on it - the secret handshake, of course. I think we all felt relieved, but I kind of missed having a mission.

"Let's play Truth or Dare," said Trish.

"Okay," I said, "I'll go first. Andrea, what do you pick? Truth or Dare?"

Andrea frowned a minute while she thought about it.

"Truth," she said.

I could have guessed that she'd pick "truth". She's not exactly the daring type.

"Tell the truth, then," I said. "Have you ever kissed a boy?"

"Oh, my gosh!" whispered Trish. "You never did, did you?"

"Does my little brother count?" asked Andrea. Trish laughed and I punched Andrea in the arm.

"Of course not," I said.

"Does it count if a boy kissed ME?" Andrea asked. Trish and I both squealed.

"When did a boy kiss you?" I asked.

"Well," said Andrea, "In first grade, Trevor Brown grabbed me on the playground and kissed me on the cheek!"

"Oh, my gosh!" I said.

"Yuk!" said Trish, and we all started giggling and making gagging noises.

"It's my turn, now!" yelled Trish when we finally got a hold on ourselves. "This is for you, Hollywood, Truth or Dare?"

I liked doing dares, so I didn't even have to think before I yelled out "Dare".

"We have to come up with a good one," said Trish.

She and Andrea huddled up and whispered a minute.

"No, she'll never do that!" said Andrea, wide-eyed.

"She has to," said Trish. "It's her dare."

"Just tell me," I said. "I'll do any dare you give me!"

I liked to think I was brave and kind of a daredevil, like Amelia Earhart, who flew a plane back when women didn't do that kind of thing, so I always did my dares in this game.

"Okay, you asked for it!" said Trish. "I dare you to go clear inside the witch's garage."

They both watched me to see if I'd chicken out. I have to admit this was a scary dare but I reminded myself that I was a brave daredevil, took a deep breath, and gave them my answer.

"All right," I said as bravely as I could. "I'll do it. I'm gonna film it for my movie, too, so people can see what a real witch's garage looks like inside."

We folded up the clubhouse and hid it away. Then we climbed up the creek bank and walked down the alley to the witch's garage. It looked just as creepy as before.

"You guys stay here and keep a lookout," I said. "Whistle real loud if you see anybody coming." I had a bad feeling about this dare.

# *8*
## INSERT SHOTS

*(Filming important objects up close so you can see them better.)*

I turned on the camera and walked toward the rickety old doors to peek in. It was kind of dark inside, and I saw lot of cobwebs. I thought about all the spiders that must live there, and wondered where the witch's one-eyed black cat was. I wasn't sure this was such a good idea.

I looked back and saw Trish and Andrea standing there watching me. Andrea was clutching Trish's arm, but Trish gave me an "OK" sign and waved me on. The camera was shaking a little because I really was scared, but I went on in.

There wasn't much in the old shack, just some boards piled in the corner and a broken-down lawn mower. Light came in through the cracks in the wall and the holes in the roof. The whole shack leaned a little to one side, and I hoped it wouldn't just fall over on top of me.

I turned around slowly, filming the inside for my movie so I could get out of there in a hurry. Suddenly I heard Trish give a loud warning whistle. Somebody was coming!

I ran outside and saw Andrea and Trish rushing to hide behind the fence across the alley. I never moved so fast in my life as I scrambled in behind them.

"Hurry!" yelled Trish.

"Shhh!" said Andrea. "That little-person homeless hobo just went past the end of the alley and looked in. I'm afraid he might have seen us!"

We stayed as quiet as mice and hoped he'd just go away. In a minute, we saw him creep up the alley. He was carrying that cigar box under his arm and looking all around as he sneaked toward the garage. We ducked lower and held our breath. With a last look around, he slipped inside the shack and we could breathe again.

"We just keep running into this guy!" I said.

"Let's just leave," said Andrea.

"What if he comes right back out?" asked Trish. "He'd catch us!"

Before we could decide what to do, the mystery guy poked his head out the doors and looked around. He scurried out and ran away, all hunched over in his layers of old clothes.

"Hey!" I said. "He didn't have the cigar box with him! He must have hidden it inside."

"Who cares?" asked Andrea. "Let's just get out of here before he comes back."

"Yeah," said Trish, nodding her head.

I know we agreed to just drop this whole thing but I really, REALLY wanted to know what was in that box. My dad always says "Curiosity killed the cat", but I can't help it. I always want to know stuff.

"I'm going back in," I said. "I have to know what's in that box! Maybe it's a clue, or maybe he has stolen jewels or something and we should tell somebody. We won't know unless we look."

"I'm really scared he'll come back," said Andrea, and she looked like she might start crying.

Trish held her hand and said, "I'm scared, too, but we're the FINS and we have to stick together through thick and thin."

I was glad I had two such good new friends.

"I'm only going to be in there a minute," I said. "Just long enough to find that cigar box and look inside. I won't even take it with me, so he'll never know, and I'll film what's inside so we have proof."

I sneaked across the alley and went back into the witch's garage. It wasn't as scary the second time, but I was afraid he'd come back so I hurried. I looked around the shack, but didn't see the box. I looked under the old lawn mower. A little green garden snake slithered out, and I let out a little scream. I'm not afraid of snakes. It just caught me by surprise.

I went over to search under the pile of boards. There were spiders and daddy long legs under there so I didn't stick my hand in, but just bent over to look. Sure enough, in the far back corner of the garage, under a board, I saw the cigar box! I turned on the camera and got it on film, and then carefully reached back there to lift out the box.

The cigar box was old, and someone had pasted a picture of a horrible looking dragon on the top. I put the box on top of the boards and slowly lifted the lid. I was finally going to see what the little-person homeless hobo guy was hiding.

Inside were six things:

1. a pocket knife with a bone handle
2. a cigarette
3. one wooden match
4. a computer disk with "killing machine" written on it
5. paper with letters and numbers on it that looked like it might be a secret code
6. a gold disc, like for a necklace, with a lightning bolt and a blue stone on it

I turned on my camera and filmed what was in the box. Then I closed it, put it back where I found it, and got out of there in a hurry.

As soon as I got out the door, Andrea and Trish started running down the alley and I was right behind them. We didn't stop running until we got to Trish's house. When we burst in the back door Trish's mom was in the kitchen.

"What are you girls up to?" she asked.

We tried to look innocent.

"Oh, nothing. Just running around for exercise," Trish said.

"Yeah," I said. "You can never get enough exercise."

Andrea just nodded.

"We're gonna play in my room for awhile," said Trish.

We walked past her mom and then ran upstairs. Trish shut the door and we all fell on the bed.

"So tell us!" she said. "Did you find the box?"

"I sure did," I said. "Look for yourself."

I played what I had filmed back through the camera, letting them watch it through the viewfinder.

"Wow!" said Andrea. "What do you suppose he's doing with that stuff?"

"It looks like he might be a spy or something, because of the secret code," said Trish.

"That's what I was thinking," I said. "And with the knife and the "Killing Machine" computer disk, maybe even a killer spy!"

"Yeah," Trish added, "Maybe that cigarette is a poison one, and the lightning-bolt necklace has secret super-powers!"

"So, now what?" Andrea asked. "We all just agreed this morning that we were gonna forget about this guy, didn't we?"

"Well," I said, "I think we need to try to follow him again, you know, to make sure he's not really breaking into people's houses or something. The stuff in the box makes me think he could be dangerous, and it's up to us to make sure he's not up to something bad. I mean, we're the only ones who know this stuff, so it's our responsibility, isn't it?"

My dad's big on responsibility. It means doing what you should.

I have to admit I was really curious now. I was just dying to follow this guy again, no matter what we agreed. Extreme curiosity has always been a fault of mine and I can't seem to get rid of it, no matter how hard I try.

Andrea and Trish looked at each other and then just shook their heads.

"I don't think we should," said Andrea.

"Neither do I," said Trish.

It was two against one.

# *9*
# ON LOCATION

*(When you film away from the
movie studio, at a real place.)*

When I got home, my mom was making peanut
butter and jelly sandwiches for lunch. I ate the crusts
first and then smashed the sandwich flat and ate the
middle. It's just something I like to do. It works better
with cheese sandwiches.

I was sitting on the front porch swing, reading a
book, when Trish came up the sidewalk, carrying a
bucket and a ball of string.

"Let's go down to the creek," she said. "I want to
show you something."

I grabbed my camera and headed back outside.

"Mom!" I yelled. "We're going down to the creek
to play!"

Trish and I ran through the alley and slid down
the creek bank. When we got to the beach area, Trish

squatted down by the water and set down the bucket and the ball of string.

"We're gonna catch some crawdads," she said.

"Crawdads?" I asked.

"Yeah," she said. "They're kind of like tiny lobsters, but we're not gonna eat them. I just like to catch them for fun."

Trish reached in her pocket and pulled out a couple of small paper clips.

"If you tie a string to a pole and put one of these on the end, the crawdad will grab it with his claw and you can pull him right out of the water!" she said.

Trish stood up and started walking away from me up the creek.

"We each have to find stick to use for a pole," she said.

I walked down the creek a little ways to look for a good stick, and that's when I saw the little-person homeless hobo guy scrambling up the bank on the other side. When he got to the top he hunched over and scurried away. I didn't even think, I just climbed up the bank and started after him.

"Hey, Hollywood!" yelled Trish from down below, "Where are you going?"

I just pointed and kept running. I didn't want to lose him.

I sneaked along behind him, down the street and through an alley. I was pretty sure he didn't know I was following him. When he crossed the street I went right after him. I thought I knew where he was going. Sure enough, he slipped through the bushes and into the same yard he where he went the last time I followed him. This time I got to the bushes right after him and turned on my camera. This time I got there in time to see him open that side basement door and actually go into the house!

# *10*
# EXPOSITION

*(When one of the characters explains a
bunch of stuff to the other characters.)*

Trish was panting when she finally caught up with me.

"What are you doing?" she asked. "You just ran off without saying anything. I almost lost you."

"Shhh!" I said. "It's the little-person homeless hobo guy. I saw him sneak right into that house! This time I'm sure of it."

"Oh, my gosh!" Trish said. "Now what?"

"Now we have to tell somebody, even if it gets us in trouble," I said, "Come with me to my house. I'm gonna tell my mom and dad and then they can call the police or something."

We ran back to my house and found my mom and dad in the back yard, working in the garden.

"Mom! Dad!" I yelled.

"What's all the excitement?" asked Dad as he got up off of his knees and brushed the dirt off his hands.

"We saw a guy break into someone's house!" I said, out of breath from running.

My mom stood up and took off her gardening gloves.

"What are you talking about? Where did you see this?" she asked.

I opened my mouth and just let it all out.

"It's kind of a long story, but we were down at the creek when this mysterious little-person homeless hobo guy came along and then later we saw him sneak into someone's basement door and I don't think it's the first time he's done this but I wasn't sure so we didn't say anything and Uncle Kurt said to just forget it but now I saw him for sure this time so you have to do something!"

I took a deep breath and waited for them to say something.

"What in the world!" exclaimed my mother. "What do you mean, a little-person homeless hobo?"

"Look," I said. "I got him on my camera!"

I turned on my camera and played back the part where he went in the side door. Mom and Dad frowned as they watched.

"You were following him?" asked my mom.

She looked upset and maybe angry.

"Honey," said my dad as he put his hand on my mother's arm, "I think the first thing to deal with is that she saw someone commit a break-in. We can sort out the rest of the story later."

He turned to me with a stern look.

"And we WILL sort this out later, young lady," he said.

When he called me "young lady" I knew I was in trouble.

"Holly, take us to the house where you saw this happen," said Dad. "Trish, you better go on home."

Trish looked relieved as she ran off, and the three of us started down the alley.

"This way," I said, leading the way. "I don't know who lives in the house, but it's on the next block."

My mother frowned.

"Holly, you know you're not supposed to leave our block without telling me. What were you thinking?"

"I don't know," I said. "I was following him and I guess I just kind of forgot."

I figured SHE wouldn't forget, though, and that I'd get in trouble for it later.

We came to the front of the house where I'd seen the hobo guy go in, and I stopped and pointed.

"I saw him go in the side door over there. I think it's a basement door like we have," I said. "He didn't see me and I ran straight home, so he's probably still in there."

"Okay," said Dad. "We're going to tell the owners right now."

We walked up the front steps and rang the doorbell. It was the kind that played a little tune. A man opened the door and I could hear a baseball game on TV somewhere in the room behind him.

"Hello," he said. "How may I help you?"

"We're the Stone family and we just moved in on the next block," said my dad, "This is Kay, I'm Michael, and this is our daughter Holly."

"Nice to meet you," said the man, "I'm George Furst and my wife Helen is in the kitchen."

"Helen!" he yelled over his shoulder, "Come meet some new neighbors!"

"This isn't a social visit," said my dad, "We think we may have an urgent situation here. Possibly a dangerous one."

Helen came up behind George, drying her hands on a dishtowel. "Dangerous?" she asked. "What's going on here?"

"Holly just saw a strange man break into your house through the side door," said my mom, pulling her cellphone out of her pocket. "We'll call the police and tell them to come right over. Until they arrive, you should get out of the house and wait on the front lawn."

Mom dialed 911.

"Oh, my gosh," gasped Helen, "I have to get Gordie!"

She ran back into the house.

"Gordie's our son," explained George, "He's eleven years old."

Helen rushed out the front door with Gordie and we all went down to the sidewalk to wait for the cops.

Gordie was a little taller than I am and he was a little pudgy. He looked really scared.

"You saw this guy?" asked Gordie, turning to me with a glare. "What were you doing spying on our house?"

"Gordie!" exclaimed his mother, "That's rude!"

I secretly agreed with her, but I tried to act nice.

"I know you didn't mean anything by it, Gordie," I said, "You're probably just upset. We all are."

Gordie just frowned.

"When the police get here, we should give them all the information we can," said my mom, "What does this guy look like, Holly, and when and where did you first see him?"

"Well, Trish and I were playing down at the creek when we first saw him," I began. "He looked like a homeless guy or a hobo or something. You know, because he was wearing layers of really old clothes that didn't fit him and that were all grungy-looking. And he was really short so we thought he must be a little person. Trish said "a midget" but I told her what you said about that not being a nice word. I don't know what kind of hair he has or anything because he always wore a hat or had his sweatshirt hood up. He walks kind of hunched over in a sneaky way, always looking around him and hiding and stuff."

"That's a really good description, Holly," said my dad. "The police will be impressed."

I was feeling pretty good after my dad said that, but then my mom spoke up.

"How did you happen to see him go into the Fursts' house?" she asked.

The good feeling went away because I knew that part of the story, the following-a-strange-man part, was going to get me into trouble, big-time.

"Well," I said, looking down at my tennies, "The second time that we saw him down at the creek we kind of followed him when he left. He was acting so sneaky we wanted to know what he was up to."

I was afraid to look at my mom, so I just kept staring at my tennies like they were the most interesting thing I'd ever seen.

"So this is the SECOND time you saw him, and you just decided to follow him here to the Fursts' house?" asked my mom.

Her voice was getting kind of high, like it does when she starts to get mad.

"Not exactly," I said. "The second time we saw him, we followed him and he went to the witch's garage."

"Witch's garage?" asked my dad. "What witch's garage?"

"You know that old worn-out house down the block with the peeling paint and the yard full of weeds and everything?" I asked. "A witch lives there with her black cat. We saw the hobo guy sneak into that shack or garage out in her back yard."

"She means Mrs. Mason's house. The Widow Mason, we call her," said Mr. Furst. He turned to look at me. "She's a poor crippled old woman who lost her husband a while back. She's just barely getting by on her Social Security, and she doesn't have money to keep up her house very well. She's certainly not a witch."

Well, you might think that I'd feel embarrassed for calling a poor old widow a witch, but I wasn't. I knew I was right and that she WAS a real witch. Of COURSE they thought she was just an old widow, that's what witches want you to think so you'll leave them alone and they can just live among us in plain sight! I didn't say anything, though, because my mom spoke up in a very stern voice.

"You're telling me that you followed this strange person off of our block, not once but THREE times?

And THIS time you even went onto someone else's property?"

"Well, actually," I said, "We followed him here into the Fursts' yard once before, but we didn't see him actually go into the house that time. Today, when we followed him, he went right in that side door. I saw him with my own eyes!"

"Holly," said my dad. My mom wasn't speaking at this point. She was just staring at me with an angry red face. "Holly, this is really too much!"

Lucky for me, a sheriff's tan car pulled up to the house at that very moment.

## *11*
## REVEAL

*(When the camera suddenly shows you something important that you couldn't see before.)*

A very tall red-haired guy about my dad's age got out of the car and walked over to us. His tan uniform looked good.

"Hello folks, I'm Sheriff Bannon," he said. "Is this where you think there may have been a break-in?"

He looked up at the house and rested his hand on his holster. "The dispatcher said someone saw a strange man entering the house. Is that right?"

"This is our house," said Mr. Furst. "Our neighbors' daughter, here, says she saw a strange man enter our side door about twenty minutes ago. They were kind enough to alert us, and we all left the house to wait for you to arrive."

"Have you seen any other activity since then?" asked Sheriff Bannon. "You didn't see him exit by any chance, did you?"

"No, nothing like that," said Mrs. Furst.

"Where does that door lead?" asked the sheriff, pointing to the side door.

"Inside the door there are steps down to the basement," said Mrs. Furst. "There are also steps leading up to the kitchen."

"You folks stay here and I'm going to check it out," said the sheriff.

He walked to the side of the house, pulled out his gun, and entered the door. After a minute he came back out.

"The basement is clear. There's no one in there. I'm going to check out the rest of the house so you all stay right here again."

And in he went again.

"He's a really good guy," said Mr. Furst to my dad, "I've known Sheriff Bannon since we were both in grade school."

"Smart as a whip!" said Mrs. Furst.

Gordie stood there kicking his foot into the dirt over and over again. He was digging a pretty good hole in the yard, but no one seemed to notice. Dad had his arm around Mom and she still looked angry. I just wished I'd disappear.

Sheriff Bannon came back out.

"The house is clear. He must have left by the back door or something, while you were out front waiting for me. He's probably just a harmless man with no place to live, but I want you to take a good look around the basement to see if anything is missing."

We all trooped in the side door and down the steps to their basement. There was a little workshop off to the right. We walked past that and the furnace and into a bigger room that had a ping-pong table in the center. Back in the corner of this room there were a couple of old lockers, like in the gym, and a rack of old clothes.

Mr. And Mrs. Furst looked all around the room.

"Nothing seems to be missing," said Mr. Furst, counting the ping-pong paddles.

"No, everything looks the same," said Mrs. Furst, as she flipped through the rack of clothing.

Something caught my eye as she pushed some of the hangers down the rack.

"Wait a minute," I said. "Wait just a minute!"

I turned on my camera and played back the part where the little-person homeless hobo guy went in their side door. I couldn't believe what I saw!

"Look at this!" I said. "Look what he's wearing."

Mr. and Mrs. Furst watched the tape with me.

"Isn't he wearing that raggedy brown jacket that's over on the rack right now?" I asked. "And that same gray sweatshirt and those big brown pants?"

I picked up a black stocking cap and some filthy tennis shoes that were lying under the rack.

"He's wearing these in the film, too," I said.

Suddenly Gordie burst into tears and ran out of the room. We could hear his feet pound up the stairs. The side door slammed with a "bang", and we all just stared at each other.

"What in the world?" asked Mrs. Furst.

Sheriff Bannon kind of smiled and shook his head. He put his hand on my shoulder.

"I think we may have found your little-person homeless hobo guy, young lady."

"Oh my gosh!" was all I could think of to say.

# *12*
# MOTIVATION

*(The character's reason for doing
something in a scene.)*

We all went outside to find Gordie. He was
sitting at the picnic table in the back yard. He had his
head down on the table, and we could see by his
shaking shoulders that he was still crying. As we got
nearer, he sat up and swiped at the tears on his face.

"Gordie," said his mother gently, "We need to
talk to you about what happened. The sheriff came all
the way over here and he deserves an explanation."

"Son," said Sheriff Bannon, "Nothing illegal
actually happened here since you just sneaked into
your own house, so I'm gonna get on back to the
station and leave you here to talk with your parents. I'm
sure they'd like to understand what you were up to, so
be honest with them. But remember that it is not a
good thing to get the police out here for nothing. It's a
waste of time while real crimes are being committed."

"I'm sorry I wasted your time, Sheriff," mumbled Gordie.

He sniffed away the last of his tears, and kind of hunched down in his seat.

"Mr. and Mrs. Furst, I'll get out of here and let you sort this all out as a family," said the sheriff.

He tipped his hat and walked around front to his car.

Mr. Furst sat at the table across from Gordie.

"Have a seat, everybody, and let's hear from Gordie," he said.

We all sat down, and Mrs. Furst slid in next to Gordie and put her arm around him.

"You really gave us all a scare, honey," said Mrs. Furst. "Why didn't you just admit it was you when Holly came to warn us about a strange man breaking into the house?"

"I was afraid you'd be mad," said Gordie. "And I guess I thought I could still keep my Secret Spy game going. I didn't think you'd find my Secret Spy outfit and blow my cover."

"Blow my cover?" Mrs. Furst raised her eyebrows. "You've been watching too much TV!"

"Son," said Mr. Furst, "Start at the beginning."

Gordie squirmed in his seat.

"I came up with the idea that I'd be a spy this summer. I'd wear a disguise and sneak around the neighborhood spying on stuff. I got some of Dad's old clothes from the rummage-sale rack in the basement and made my Secret Spy outfit so if anyone saw me they wouldn't know I was just a kid."

"Why didn't you just ask for the clothes?" asked his mother. "I would have given them to you for a spy outfit."

"Mo-om!" said Gordie. "Then it wouldn't have been secret! You would have known."

"Oh, Gordie," sighed his mom. "You've got to get over this spy obsession."

"Anyway, said Gordie. "I'd just sneak down into the basement, get dressed in my Secret Spy outfit, and go out the side door."

"That's not so bad, I guess," said his dad. "But I'm concerned about another thing. Tell me about your going into someone else's property."

Gordie looked down at the table. "Oh, you mean the witch's garage."

"The Widow Mason's garage, yes," said Mr. Furst. "I'm talking about your going in there without her permission. You know better than that! What were you thinking?"

"Well," said Gordie, "I was thinking I needed a Secret Spy headquarters of some kind, and I figured that it'd be a great one since no one ever goes in it 'cause they're scared of the witch!"

He looked kind of proud of this idea, but I could see that his parents didn't think much of it. They looked at each other and frowned.

"Young man, you're grounded for a week," said Mr. Furst. "You won't be leaving the house at all unless it's with us. And I don't want you playing on other people's property without their permission ever again. Do you understand me?"

"Yes, sir," said Gordie sheepishly.

"Now, Holly," said Mrs Furst, "While you were following our son, did you see anything else you think we should know about? I want everything cleared up right now."

I looked at Gordie and thought about his hidden cigar box. He frowned at me like he could tell what I was thinking.

I know how important it is for a kid to have SOME secrets. I have a secret hiding place of my own, a metal box that my mom and dad gave me. It has a built-in number lock, and I'm the only one who knows the combination to open it.

"No, Mrs. Furst," I said, "I don't have anything else to tell you."

"Well," said Mr. Furst as he got up from the table. "We're sorry about all this. We're sorry Gordie caused you a scare. Thanks a lot for being such good neighbors by coming over to warn us about what you saw."

"We're just glad it was nothing serious," said my dad as he helped Mom up from the table.

"And it was very nice meeting you," said my mom. "We'll have to have you over after Gordie's done being grounded."

"See you, Gordie," I said.

He gave me a weak little wave. He was in for a long week. We headed off for home.

"Holly," said my mother sternly, "You have some explaining to do when we get home."

I had forgotten about that for a minute. I was in trouble, too.

# *13*
# HIATUS

*(When the film company takes a
few days off from filming.)*

It turns out my parents weren't too keen on my following around a strange man. The fact that I'd left the block, without telling my mom first, only made it worse. They grounded me for a week. If I'd told them that I also went into somebody else's property, like the witch's garage, I'd probably STILL be grounded!

I spent some of the long week reading because I like to, and some of it helping around the house because my mom and dad made me, as part of my punishment. I thought about Gordie who was stuck at home, as well, and wondered what he was doing. I thought about Andrea and Trish and hoped they weren't having a FINS meeting without me. I wasn't even allowed to talk to them on the phone.

I wrote my Uncle Kurt a long E-mail and told him about the whole adventure. He wrote back and was pretty nice about it, although he kind of said "I told you so".

I spent some time working on my movie, "My New Hometown." I used Dad's super-duper computer to edit the stuff I shot with my video camera.

When I edit, I put together the parts I like in the order I want them. I also take out any parts I don't like, like when I got the camera stuck in the bushes at Gordie's house. All you could see, for a minute there, was a jerky picture of branches and leaves and stuff. After I did the editing, I added in the sound of my voice, telling people more about what they were seeing on the film. The voice part is called a "voice over". I also set up the camera in my bedroom and filmed myself, where I talked right to the camera about my new home town. I put that in the movie here and there to tie it all together.

I actually make a script for my movies. I learned how from my mom's friend Susan, back in LA. She's a documentary filmmaker which means she makes movies about real things, not make-believe movies like you see in the theater or on TV. That's the kind of filmmaker I am, too, at least for now. Here's what the script looks like

| PICTURE | SOUND |
|---|---|
| Shots of Holly talking to the camera. | "I'm going to show you my new home town, called Lebanon, Indiana." |
| Shots of us unpacking on moving day. | Voice Over-"Our new house is really great but moving in was a lot of work." |
| Shots of Holly's room. | Voice Over-"I love my new room." |
| Shots of the 4th of July Parade. | Voice Over-"On the 4th of July a parade went down my very own street. Look at all the floats!" |

Anyway, you get the idea. It's a lot of work, but when you're done the movie makes sense and everybody gets what you're trying to say.

I'm not supposed to brag, but back in L.A. in the 4th grade I won a prize for Best Art Project with my movie called "Adopt A Pet". I went to the dog pound and to the greyhound rescue place and to pet stores and stuff to film that one. I just love making movies!

I guess getting grounded for a week gave me the time to pretty much finish my movie, which was a good thing. It just needed a snazzy ending and I hadn't quite figured that out yet.

# *14*
# PICK-UP SHOTS

*(When you go back to film something*
*important, that you forgot to show before.)*

On the day I was finally un-grounded, I jumped out of bed and dressed in a big hurry. I couldn't wait to get out of the house and go see Trish and Andrea.

I called them both on the phone, and we agreed we'd meet in our clubhouse under the bridge at nine o'clock sharp. Whoever got there first was supposed to set up the clubhouse. The FINS were back in business!

I ate a bowl of oatmeal with raisins as fast as I could. When I finished I put my dishes in the sink, grabbed my camera, and ran out to go to the creek.

"Don't you dare leave the block!" yelled my mother as I left.

"I won't," I said over my shoulder.

When I got to our place under the bridge, Trish was just putting up the clubhouse so I helped her. Andrea got there right when we finished. We all hugged each other before we crawled inside the clubhouse. It seemed like we hadn't seen each other forever!

"The FINS meeting will now come to order!" I said.

We all did the handshake.

"We still need to come up with a secret password," said Trish. "We need a word you have to say before we let you into the clubhouse, so we know it's a member and not someone else."

"How about the word "gills"?" I asked. "That might be a good password since fish use them to breathe and it goes pretty good with FINS."

"That'll work," said Trish. "Let's vote on it."

We voted on it, and it was three "for" and zero "against" so GILLS it was.

"Look what I brought," said Andrea.

She opened her backpack and pulled out a bag of goldfish crackers.

"I think these should be our official FINS food," she said.

It was a great idea. It was the perfect food for us. I filmed Andrea and Trish eating some goldfish.

"What do you want to do now?" asked Trish.

She kind of mumbled because she had a mouth full of crackers.

"Let's work on the front yard," said Andrea. "We'll make a garden for the clubhouse."

So we crawled out and started picking up rocks to make a border around our yard. I went over to the bank and started picking some flowering weeds for our garden. I found Queen Ann's Lace, which had lacy white flowers, and goldenrod, which had little yellow flowers. We finished the rock border and I was filming Trish and Andrea planting the flowers when I saw Gordie slide down the bank across the creek.

"Hey, Gordie!" I yelled. "Hi!"

"What are you guys doing?" he asked.

"Come on over and we'll show you," I said.

He started looking for a place where he could cross the creek on some stepping stones so he wouldn't get too wet.

"Who's that?" asked Trish.

"Oh, my gosh!" I said, "I forgot you guys don't know yet! Gordie is the little-person homeless-hobo guy we were following."

"Honest?" asked Andrea, "You mean it was just a kid?"

"It was Gordie, all right," I replied. "He was wearing his dad's old clothes for a disguise so he could be a Secret Spy. He got grounded for a week, too."

Gordie made it across the creek and joined us in front of the clubhouse.

"Gordie, these are my friends Andrea and Trish," I said. "Guys, this is Gordie."

"Nice to meet you," said Gordie politely. "What are you guys up to?"

"We're just making a front yard and a garden," said Trish.

"Well, it's a cool little house," said Gordie. "It'd make a great clubhouse."

We just looked at each other but didn't say anything, since our club was supposed to be a secret.

"How's it feel to be un-grounded?" I asked. "You know, I got grounded for a week, too."

"You did?" asked Gordie. "Then you know how it feels. Even worse than that, though, is that I'm never ever allowed back in the witch's garage, which was my Secret Spy headquarters."

"I guess you'll just have to find a new secret hideout," I said. "Every spy needs one."

"Yeah, I guess I will, but I had my most important spying tools hidden in there. It looks like I'll never be able to get them back, and I won't be much of a Secret Spy without them."

He looked like he might actually cry or something.

"You mean the stuff in the cigar box?" Trish asked.

Gordie looked shocked. "You know about that?"

"Yeah," I said, "We saw you carry it around and then leave it in the witch's garage, so I went in there after you left one day and found it."

"Did you take it?" he asked with a frown.

"No," I said. "We know what's inside though. We thought it looked like spy stuff, maybe Killer Spy stuff. What were those things for, anyway?"

Gordie shook his head. "I can't tell you. They're secret."

I was dying of curiosity. I really wanted to know. Then I figured out how to get him to tell.

"You know, Gordie," I said, "My parents never told ME I couldn't go back into the witch's garage - probably because they never found out I went in there in the first place. But anyway, I could go back in and get it out for you."

He broke into a big grin. "Would you?" he asked, "That'd be just great!"

"I will," I said. "If you tell us what all the things inside were for."

He didn't look too happy about that.

"We can keep a secret," Andrea said.

"Yeah," added Trish, "We have a big secret of our own that we're keeping."

I knew she meant our secret FINS club.

"Well, okay," said Gordie slowly. "I guess it'd be okay. I really, really need my stuff back. But you have to promise, hope to die, that you won't tell anyone else."

"We promise," I said right away. "Let's go get it right now, before the witch or somebody finds it first."

We scrambled up the creek bank and headed over to the witch's house.

"You know the drill," I said when we arrived. "You guys keep a lookout while I go in."

I was in and out of there in a flash this time, since I already knew where the cigar box was hidden. Gordie reached out to take the box from me, but I pulled it back.

"Uh-uh," I said, shaking my head. "I'll hold it while you tell us what all this stuff is for. That's the deal."

Gordie looked up and down the alley. "We can't just do this out here in the open! That stuff's Top Secret! Someone might come along and see us."

"Let's do it in the clubhouse," said Andrea.

I poked her in the ribs, hard.

"In the cardboard house, you mean," I said with a stern look. She wasn't supposed to mention the secret club to outsiders, but Gordie didn't seem to even notice what she'd said. I guess he was too excited about getting his Secret Spy stuff back.

# *15*
# THAT'S A WRAP!

*(What the assistant director says when the
filming's done and everyone should go home.)*

We all ran back to the creek and crawled into
the clubhouse.

I have to say, it looked pretty great with the new
yard and with the garden we'd just planted. Once we
were all seated in a circle, I put the cigar box on my lap
and opened the lid. Everything was still there like
before.

"Tell us about the knife," I said, picking up the
pocket knife with the bone handle.

"My best friend traded me that knife for my two
best Transformer cards," said Gordie. "I figured a spy
needed one, but I knew my parents probably wouldn't
let me keep it so I hid it in here. I haven't ever used it
yet, but you never know when you'll need one."

"You are one really sneaky spy!" said Trish.

I could tell she was impressed.

"You don't smoke, do you?" I asked, picking up the cigarette and the wooden match.

"No, of course not," said Gordie. "What happened was I was snooping through my dad's top dresser drawer one day. That's his junk drawer, and he has all sorts of neat things in there. I found this clear glass tube that had one cigarette and one wooden match inside it somehow. There was no way to open the tube, so I didn't know how somebody got them in there in the first place. I was trying to figure it out when I dropped the tube and the glass broke. I cleaned up the glass, but figured I had to hide what was inside so my dad wouldn't find out I'd been snooping."

Andrea looked a little shocked.

"You would be in so much trouble!" she said.

"I know," said Gordie, "That's why I hid them in here."

"My mom has one of those glass tubes with the cigarette and match sealed inside," said Trish. "A friend of hers gave it to her as a joke when she quit smoking last year. It came with a piece of paper that said, "In case of emergency, break glass", like on the fire extinguisher boxes at school. Your dad probably used to smoke."

"It must have been before I was born," said Gordie, "I've never seen him smoke and my parents both say how bad it is for you."

We all nodded. Our parents had said the same thing.

"This computer disk had us worried," I said, taking the "Killing Machine" disk out of the box. "This and the knife made us think you were a Killer Spy, instead of just a regular spy."

"Oh, that!" said Gordie with a smile. "That's just a copy of a really cool computer game that my friend gave me. My mom won't let me buy computer games like this because she thinks they're too violent. I can't really ever play it on my computer at home, though, because she might come in and catch me with it, so I just keep it here."

"Why do you have a necklace?" I asked. I picked up the gold disc with a lightning bolt and a blue stone on it. "Isn't that a girl thing?"

"It's not a necklace," said Gordie. "It's a magic medal, and it gives me my Super Spy powers. I found it in the creek and cleaned it up."

"Cool," said Trish, "Can I touch it?"

"Sure," he said, "It only works for me, anyway."

We all handed it around. The last thing in the box was the piece of paper with the code on it.

"How does this code work?" I asked.

"Look," said Gordie. "Each number is lined up with a letter from the alphabet. To write a note in secret code you just write the number that stands for each letter you want to use, and no one can read it unless they have this code key!"

We all looked at the code and saw how it worked. The number 1 stood for A, 2 was B, 3 was C, and so on.

"This is great!" I said. "We could use this in our secret club!"

Andrea and Trish gasped.

"Secret club?" asked Gordie. "What secret club?"

I knew I'd messed up. Andrea and Trish looked worried.

"What do you think, guys?" I asked them. "Gordie shared his secret spy stuff with us. Do you think we should tell him our secret in return?"

We all turned to look at Gordie. He got a serious look on his face, probably trying to look trustworthy so we'd tell him.

"Hold your ears, Gordie," said Trish. "We have to talk in secret a minute."

He held his ears and we all leaned in to whisper.

"If we tell him," said Trish, "It won't be a secret club anymore."

She had a point there. I thought about it a minute and came up with an idea.

"There IS a way we could tell him and still have it be a secret club," I said.

"How's that?" asked Andrea.

"If we made him a member after we told him!" I said. "Then it would still be a secret club, and we'd have four members instead of three." I was getting excited about this idea. "It might be good to have such a sneaky Secret Spy in the club."

"She's right," said Trish. "He's the sneakiest person I know AND he's really nice. See, look at him. He's still holding his ears like we told him to."

We looked over at Gordie. He was still holding his ears, and he was even humming quietly to make sure he wouldn't hear us through his hands.

"Let's do it!" said Trish.

"Yeah!" agreed Andrea.

"You can uncover your ears, now!" I yelled at Gordie.

We explained all about the secret club to Gordie. We told him how FINS stood for "Friends In Need Society" and we gave him the secret password, "gills". Then we showed him the secret handshake. We changed it a little, now that we had a new member. Instead of giving three wrist shakes and three finger shakes we made it four shakes, since there were four members now.

And that's how we became the Four FINS. I still had my camera with me, so after we made Gordie an official member I got us all on film together. I set the camera up on the stump under the bridge and pointed it at the FINS, standing in our nice new yard in front of the clubhouse. I turned the camera on and ran over to stand in the middle of them. We all waved like crazy at the camera and then we yelled, "Welcome to My New Hometown!" It made a really snazzy ending for my movie!

THAT'S A WRAP!

**LINDA ROCKSTROH** is a filmmaker in Hollywood and a former English teacher. She lives with two indoor cats & lots of outdoor wildlife on her property in Los Angeles including bobcats, deer, skunks, raccoons, coyotes, & hummingbirds. She loves mysteries, swimming, and making ceramics.